A Hot Cup of Chocolate

untington Public Library
145 Pidgeon Hill Road
Station, NY 11746

An Imprint of Starfish Bay Publishing Pty Ltd
www.starfishbaypublishing.com

A HOT CUP OF CHOCOLATE

Copyright © 2016 by Rose Stanley and Lisa Allen
First North American edition Published by Starfish Bay Children's Books in 2016
ISBN: 978-1-76036-019-1
Published by arrangement with Duck Creek Press, Auckland, New Zealand
Printed and bound in China by Beijing Zhongke Printing Co., Ltd
Building 101, Songzhuang Industry Zone, Beijing 101118

This book is copyright.
Apart from any fair dealing for the purpose of private study, research, criticism or review, as permitted under the Copyright Act, no part of this publication may be reproduced or transmitted in any form or by any means without the prior written permission of the publisher.
All Rights Reserved.

Rose Stanley worked as a Student Support Specialist in a New Zealand primary school for six years and has most recently been an advisor for the Lifewalk Trust, where she trains volunteers working in a similar support role. Her work has involved supporting many children as they have gone through difficult life experiences, including bereavement, family separations, and friendship problems. She has also written a number of articles for the parenting magazine *Tots to Teens*.

Lisa Allen is a New Zealand graphic designer and freelance illustrator. She also paints on commission and teaches art. Lisa has illustrated a number of successful picture books for Duck Creek Press, as well as *Mangrove* and *Anzac Day Parade* for Penguin Books.

Also by Rose Stanley and Lisa Allen

A Hot Cup of Chocolate

By Rose Stanley

Illustrated by Lisa Allen

Johan adored a good cup of hot chocolate.

Creamy, milky hot chocolate... yum!

Was there anything better in the whole wide world?

When he came home from a cold, wet day at school,
his mom would say, “How about a hot chocolate, Johan?
That’ll make you feel better!”
He would snuggle up in a blanket, play cards
with his sister Lanie, and dip gingersnap into his
mug of chocolaty, dreamy delight.

Early on Saturday mornings in the winter, when it was
frosty and freezing and he was off to play football,
he would stand on a chair and heat his chocolate
in the microwave, and then pour it into a thermos
so he could sip at it in the car, savoring every mouthful.

BIX

If Mom or Dad were sick with a cold, Johan loved to tell them to, "Sit down, and I'll get you a hot chocolate!" And they would always say, "Mmmm, that is so good!"

And when Lanie, who was four and totally besotted with ducks and swans, was in one of her painful moods, he would pick her up and say, "What comes in a cup and makes me happy?" She would loudly scream "Chocolate!" and drag him by the hand to the fridge as she tried to help him make her one.

But sometimes her help was a bit of a disaster.
Like the time she missed the cup and spilled milk
down the side of the counter and onto their dog, Muffy,
whose fur was really long and got tangled easily.
Muffy howled and raced round and round the kitchen,
flicking hot chocolate mixed with dirt from his coat
everywhere and boy did he stink!
So then Johan had to give him a bath.
A very long, soapy bath.
Mom was not happy, and neither was Johan.
Sisters!

Johan's friend, Henry, often came around to play
after school and he loved hot chocolate, too.
Johan would make a cup for each of them for
an afternoon snack.

Actually, he had a feeling that Henry didn't get much
hot chocolate made for him at his house, and maybe not
much of anything else either.

Henry didn't talk much about his home or his
family, and he didn't seem to have too much trouble talking
his mom into letting him stay longer at Johan's house.

One afternoon, Henry was around at Johan's place again, and he didn't seem to be in a very good mood. At lunchtime, one of the boys had said something to him as a joke, but Henry didn't think it was very funny. He said bad things to the boy and then chased him around the playground with a really angry expression on his face.

Lots of the kids thought it was funny, but Johan watched the scared look on the boy's face, and he knew it wasn't a joke to him.

And now, as they sipped their hot chocolate, Henry wasn't talking and laughing with Johan. Johan was trying to be careful not to say the wrong thing, and Henry just kept asking, "Can I stay at your place for a sleepover tonight?"

Johan went to ask his mom if that was okay,
but mom was on the phone, had been for ages,
and instead of laughing and smiling like she did
when she talked to her friends, she was talking
very quietly and seriously.

Johan stood at the door and waited for a while,
but mom threw him one of those "Not now, Johan!"
looks, and he snuck back to the kitchen.

"Where's mom?" asked his little sister Lanie, holding onto her smelly old toy ducky.

Johan loved to tease Lanie about throwing Ducky away someday because he was so old and gross, but Lanie would just hold onto him even more tightly and cover his non-existent ears, saying, "Don't listen to him, my poor ducky!"

“She’s on the phone,” said Johan, picking her up and dumping her playfully on the couch. “So don’t disturb her, or she’ll get grumpy, and we all know what happens then!” Lanie smiled and took the banana Johan handed to her. “Okay,” she said and went back to her puzzle. “Want to help me?” She looked over at Henry and handed him a piece of the puzzle.

Henry looked bored, but then he said, “I guess so… even if you do have banana breath!” and he pretended to vomit, making really disgusting noises.

Lanie laughed and laughed, and Johan noticed that Henry seemed to be secretly enjoying it.

Then he pretended that the puzzle was too hard and he needed Lanie’s help. Lanie said, “Boy, for a big kid you don’t know much about birds, do you Henry?”

When Mom did finally get off the phone, Henry and Johan had done the same Birds of the World puzzle five times over with Lanie and given her "horsey" rides until their backs caved in.

They were just about to ask if Henry could stay when Mom said, “Henry, we’d love to have you stay for dinner and the night if you would like to.”

Henry’s face lit up like he had just been given his own private jet, and he said, “You bet! Thanks Mrs. G!”

And just like that, Henry was in the best mood ever. For the rest of the night Johan didn't have to be careful what he said, and they had a heap of fun together.

They watched their favorite program *Munched Within Moments* with Johan's dad and then played their own version of it by dive-bombing each other on the couch.

Then they gave Lanie a couple more goes at her
“horsey” rides and did extreme jumps over the bean bags,
which made her so hyper that Johan’s dad said,
“I think it’s time for bed, Lanie!” and threw her over his
shoulder to take her upstairs to her room.
Boy, did she get grumpy!
Then finally, just before bed, Johan’s mom let them
make a cup of chocolate with two marshmallows in each
and a piece of her homemade caramel slice.
Henry said, “This is the best
night of my whole life!”
That made Johan feel good.

Once they had talked until they couldn't stay awake, the last thought that went through Johan's head was how weird it was that Mom knew, before he had asked her, that he wanted Henry to stay over. She normally needed a lot more persuading than that!

When the boys got to school that morning, they had only been in class a little while when Henry got called up to the office on the intercom.

He was away for the whole first block, and when he came back in time for recess he didn't want to talk about what he'd been doing. All he said was, "It's family stuff. You know..." and grinned at Johan, grabbing the football from him and taking off at top speed toward the field.

So Johan tried not to ask questions, but the next day Henry told him that his mom and dad were not going to live together anymore and that it was okay because all they did was argue anyway.

Over the next few weeks, Henry had good days and bad days. On good days, they would laugh and joke and play football and everything was all good.

But on bad days, Johan would be more careful around Henry and make sure he didn't say anything that would get Henry mad. All the kids knew to stay away from Henry when he was mad.

On his bad and mad days, Henry would often disappear from class and talk to someone up in the office building.

RECEIVED 2 9 2016

DISCARD

On his bad days, Henry would sometimes ask to come to Johan's place. And Johan would say, "I'll ask my mom." And every now and then as they walked in the door and dropped their bags in a heap on the floor, Henry would say, "My turn to make the hot chocolate!"